HEY BOY

I0617898

HEY BOY

A. W. W. BREMONT

QUEER MOJO
A Rebel Satori Imprint
New Orleans

Published in the United States of America by
REBEL SATORI PRESS
www.rebelsatori.com

This is a work of fiction. Names, characters, places, and incidents are the product of the author's imagination and are used fictitiously and any resemblance to actual persons, living or dead, business establishments, events, or locales is entirely coincidental. The publisher does not have any control over and does not assume any responsibility for author or third-party websites or their content.

Library of Congress Control Number:2019953958

A could barely keep his eyes open strangely enough and a grey hoodie ungirdled was sustained gently behind him by the filthy midnight air and there he was and in trying not to scream and wail he suddenly fell victim to the annoying pondering of the differences or non differences between the burden of futility and the burden of contempt and it was all quite stupid and useless and irrelevant to him and he surely would never have cared at all to ask what the fuckitty fuck fuck makes Iago quote unquote evil and he was dozing off and losing grip of the volume he was supposed to be reading for the term paper he was supposed to be writing due later today while his yellow and thin and soft and straight as fuck and silky smooth and delicate bangs moved back and forth hiding his deep ocean blue eyes that were a blue million miles and those yellow and thin and soft and straight as fuck and silky smooth and delicate bangs that were moving back and forth were also hiding most of his bloodless and alabaster and skeletal and almost translucent face which matched the rest of his waif like and skeletal as well and utterly hairless and bright as a Nazi lamp shade frame and he was in front of his MacBook Pro where his Spotify was saying, youre so like a rose youre so like a rose youre so like a rose, and where he had been looking at web sites dedicated to photography and a few to design some two hours previous and all the while trying not to think about the thing no one but himself and two other human specimens as of yet at least knew about and it was as well the kind of thing he had thought he had determined or something he would not engage in once he had finally gotten to New York and it was also the thing that had happened three hours ago or so and the fucking kind of fucking thing a few months ago he had kind of vowed or whatever the fuck to himself he would never take part in again but had

2

just done with now inside himself in his guts feeling the usual and mandatory loathing of the self which of fucking course was that anciently developed and tilled and cared for and strengthened and preserved and fed loathing of the self present at every motherfucking second including just now and including still at this very moment and all of which meant he could not take the Skype video call from Eve and Illona which was buzzing since he knew they definitely would see something in him and he sure as fuck did not want them to see that in him and they would look and smile at each other like accomplices and then they would proceed to fucking torture him by asking passive aggressive and seemingly harmless questions about what had he done lately and other fucking stupid shit like that until he had no other option but to fucking confess and he sure as fuck did not want all that fucking shit to happen and therefore preferred to choose to pretend to continue or pretend to try to continue reading the fucking book and that was a matter that was becoming more and more pressing by the hour and by the minute and by the fucking second because the fucking term paper was due in eight hours and he could not afford to fail yet another

class and most certainly not this very specific class
yet again because that could very fucking probably
result in him getting expelled or some shit like
that or so he thought and that was something he
highly doubted he wanted to happen to him since
it would mean less means and possibilities to be
able to some day pay the gargantuan amount of
dough he owed in student loans and in order to
stop thinking about that he got up and put the
fucking book aside and Silverchair were saying,
for as long as youre here were not you make the
sound of laughter and sharpened nails seem softer
and i need you now somehow and i need you now
somehow open fire on the needs designed on my
knees for you open fire on my knees desires what i
need from you, and he walked towards his closet
and opened it and admired and touched all those
items he loved so fucking much and in his
extremely highly regarded by himself opinion
were one of the few things that made existence
almost bearable and not so extremely unworthy
and these things included all the Slimane and
American Eagle Super Skinny Jeans with this
specific piece of attire, the Super Skinny Jeans
being a style of clothing items sometime in the
now very distant past he had called stupid and

before that considered the only things he would
be willing and interested in wearing on his lower
body and then he moved on to admire and touch
all the long coats and all the Saint Laurent t shirts
and all the Aeropostale hoodies and then he
walked towards his drawers and opened them and
they were replete with Calvin Klein and American
Eagle boxer briefs and took a good look and sniff
at all these things and it felt good because they all
smelled of Bleu De Chanel Eau De Parfum
because what the fuck if such a considerable
amount of the jerks he used to see liked to spend
fucktons of money on him so fucking be it and he
was the one whom since he was a small kid with
his cherry lips and golden locks he could make
grown men and women gasp when he went
walking past them and in his hot pants and it was
great buying all those bottles of one hundred and
fifty milliliters of Bleu De Chanel Eau De Parfum
and look at those beautiful posters of the Great
Gaspard also known as the movie version of Yves
Saint Laurent ad and it was great buying all those
bottles of fifty milliliters of Opium Eau De
Parfum Pour Homme as well and the jerks loved
to see him in those underpants and there was even
more dough when he was willing to do all those

other things and when he was willing to as they used to say cross what they used to call his boundaries all of this even though he never really knew for sure or cared about at all just what exactly in the fuck that meant and much less if he had any to speak of, though that was not something he really gave a fucking shit about or so he thought and even though he hated every second of it it was all that vodka and all those Xannies and all that Valium and all those Percs and all that blow and all those yummy Oxys and all that Mrs O and all that Nembutal and all the Molly which was of course always the one he liked the least and the most fucking boring of them all and all those Wafers what were always worth it besides all the fucking money and they were all worth every single anal tear which most of the time bled like mothefuckers and every single HPV scare and every single HIV scare and every single hour spent tied up and every bruise and every single cut and every single mark and every single fucking burn and every single scratch and every single loss of blood and every single clamping and every single motherfucking piercing and every single fucking time his face ended up completely covered in and dripping with jerk or family man cum or housewife squirt and every time he had to end up having to walk all the fucking way to the E R at fucking four fucking thirty in the morning or every time he was forced to drink his piss or eat his shit or motherfucking dog shit or lick the shit out of the asshole of jerk or of a bitch and every time he was forced to jerk dogs off and eat the cum afterwards and every time he was forced to drink piss out of a dog's bowl and all the times he spent up to seventy two hours inside a gimp cunting suit or every single time his back and his ass cheeks ended up dripping with blood after hours of whipping or some fucking utter bullshit like that and every single time his mouth was so filled with cum he had to swallow and every single time he had to deal with the ones who needed to punch him in the face until there were bruises and blood coming out of his mouth so they could cum which incidentally almost always were amongst the ones that gave him the heftiest tips and paid very well and then they would kiss him for like ten minutes but they also needed to punch him in the balls and A was even less enthusiastic about that or so he thought at the time because the jerks paid so well even after treating him like a dog or much much much motherfucking worse and anyway everything and anything was and would be much better than that one specific time and after a few years some of his fuck buddies started fucking nagging him to stop doing it but what the fuck did they know since they were fucking starving artists which meant that if they knew shit about anything they most definitely and surely would not fucking be starving fucking artists to begin with and especially with so many of them being so pretty and he was going to graduate fucking high fucking school and leave all that motherfucking and disgusting suburban bullshit cage of depression and murder and suicide and death behind for good and he did not want ever again to hear how that place would tell him it is over and that he belonged to it and that it filled his mouth with dirt and to fucking relax because it is all fucking over and that he could never leave and that it took his second digit with it and he was going to apply for that partial scholarship at Berkeley which he was sure as fuck was going to get and he was going to start over or some of those clichéd idiocies most of the imbecilic human specimens say in situations like that and say something like, so long iowa go fuck yourself hello new york, and then go to some secluded place in the outskirts of his suburb and give both middle fingers to those suburbs he had spent the last eight fucking years or so living in or some clichéd idiocy like that most of the imbecilic human specimens do in situations like that but before that he had to actually finish fucking high fucking school and apply for that motherfucking Berkeley partial scholarship and wait and receive the letter which he knew would say he had been accepted and read it and quit his stupid pseudo job at motherfucking Target and which was an action that obviously caused the dismay of lots and fucking lots of idiots including the bitches club to which he belonged to and to which besides himself also belonged his school friends Carrie and Ulrike and Natalie or just Nat and Tammy and Sam whose full name was Samantha and all of whom insisted on taking him out on a special goodbye bar and club hopping night and of that fucking special goodbye bar and club hopping night the best and highest and most memorable point as far as A was concerned was by very fucking far when he smoked nine cigarettes all at the same time which of course included A posing for a photograph and insisting Carrie took one with his own iPhone even though he had never thought at all Carrie could be able to actually take a barely decent photograph but what the fuck and he had to turned down three fucking thousand fucking dollar offers to travel as a slave to some very serious and professional dungeons in Dubai and Riyadh and London and Houston and D C and Berlin and Tokyo and Baghdad and Kabul and he also had to quit his midnight part time stripper gig which caused even more woe among even more people that were even more idiotic and was something which obviously he could not give a shit about if a life long free supply of Oxys depended on it and he had also to say so long to a very select and small group of the jerks which were some of the ones who always paid the most and were less of a nuisance and usually did not do shit like treat him like an animal or fist his asshole that frequently or try to anyway or do their best to make him bleed as much as possible through various and diverse methods or caused him anal tears which most of the time bled like mothefuckers and rarely gave him reasons for HPV scares or for HIV scares and did not usually tie him up for many hours and did not leave that many bruises or cuts or marks or fucking burns or too many scratches and never caused him to lose that much blood and did not use that many clamps on him and such clamps were not that painful and they were not left on his nipples or his cock or his balls or his navel or his arms or his chest or his thighs for too fucking long and almost never or somewhat rarely pierced his nipples or his cock or his balls or his navel or his arms or his chest or his thighs with needles or whatever the fuck they had at hand and almost never left him having to walk all the fucking way to the E R at fucking four fucking thirty in the morning or never or almost never forced him to drink his piss or eat his shit or motherfucking dog shit or lick the shit out of their assholes or forced him to jerk dogs off and eat the cum afterwards or forced him to drink piss out of the bowl of a dog or never made him spend up to seventy two hours inside a gimp cunting suit or almost never made his back and his ass cheeks end up dripping with blood after hours of whipping or some fucking utter bullshit like that or they were not among the ones who needed to punch him in the face until there were bruises and blood coming out of his mouth so they could cum or very rarely forced him to go with them to dark rooms for bug chasers and many other shit but instead indulged him in every whim like all the fucking one hundred and fifty milliliters bottles of Bleu De Chanel Eau De Parfum being every time so fucking nice to take a good and positively long look at the posters of the Great Gaspard also known as the movie version of Yves Saint Laurent ad they had at the store and then he started with the goodbyes to some of his now ex fuck buddies and in one of such occasions knowing as he was leaving that that one in particular was actually fucking crying afterwards and which was precisely the kind of bullshit he couldn't give a shit about if a life long free supply of Oxys depended on it and yet right now he couldn't stop thinking about the starving artists who were always smoking fucking Marlboros twenty four seven three fucking hundred and fucking sixty five and that very obviously was practically the only thing they could do besides skating or smoking pot and maybe sometimes dealing a bit since no human specimen ever lowered themselves enough to look at them and certainly much less to look at one of those fucking utter pieces of shit they made and tried to sell and even much, much less actually buy one or more of them or even worse to throw them some fucking change and there never had been anyone to give all those starving artists that calm and haughty look that damns all those other human specimens around them and their pieces of shit artworks and he remembered how in the months previous to his departure to New York two of them had been found dead, one who was thirteen years old in an alley who had apparently bit it from an intentional crank overdose and the other one a fourteen year old one who had been found in one of the rooms of this abandoned and crumbling and completely fucked up building some people used to go to to get fucked up on booze and all other kinds of substances until total impairment struck and to fuck and to deal and score and sleep and listen to music and engage in the occasional animal torture and sacrifice which most times consisted of beating the living shit out of fucking cats and dogs of all ages and kicking and spitting on the things and then taking knives or a knife and very thoroughly skinning them alive while hysterically and maniacally and laughing out loud at the incredibly loud sounds of pure and total agony the things vociferated and also at the sound the very skinning produced which was like tearing a dress or a pair of pants or a coat apart which was then followed by the things getting nailed to wood boards attached to the walls sometimes after setting them on fire while still alive but only sometimes and in various other forms of recreation and it had been the case that an anonymous caller had notified the police six days after the sorry bastard had bit it and that had been maybe because no one had noticed before or maybe because no one had particularly cared or noticed before and before the police arrived the people who saw the shattered and bloody and ripped apart and shapeless mess that was the putrid thing that remained of what once had been the sorry bastard and that kind of looked like the T Hyphen One Thousand in Terminator Two Colon Judgment Day the last time it manages to surface and shriek and fling its arms around or what is left of them after the T Hyphen Eight Hundred shots him with a grenade launcher causing him to fall into a vat of molten steel were quick to take their phones out and take pictures and laugh and say things like, thats gotta hurt, and, ew, and, ouch hah, and when the police arrived the stench was quite remarkable and the shattered and bloody and ripped apart and shapeless mess that was the putrid thing that remained of what once had been the sorry bastard and that kind of looked like the T Hyphen One Thousand in Terminator Two Colon Judgment

Day the last time it manages to surface and shriek and fling its arms around or what is left of them after the T Hyphen Eight Hundred shots him with a grenade launcher causing him to fall into a vat of molten steel was there completely surrounded by smashed beer and moonshine bottles and used and broken syringes and bloody razor blades and shitloads of bloody needles and shit and piss and vomit and cum and remains of crack and H and crank and used condoms and it was precisely this one last detail the one that was the more baffling and flabbergasting with these last particular items turning out to be a very peculiar surprise to be found there since the very vast majority of the dudes who fucked there were most positively not the kind of dudes who were prone to bother to perform the actions of buying or asking for or stealing or keeping or using condoms and it seemed that the shattered and bloody and ripped apart and shapeless mess that was the putrid thing that remained of what once had been the sorry bastard and that kind of looked like the T Hyphen One Thousand in Terminator Two Colon Judgment Day the last time it manages to surface and shriek and fling its arms around or what is left of them after the T Hyphen Eight

Hundred shots him with a grenade launcher causing him to fall into a vat of molten steel had been severely punched and hit and bashed many many many fucking times with a very big and strong and heavy object or objects which accounted for its utterly smashed skull and the way its brains were splattered all fucking over as well as its busted left blue eye dangling from its socket and the corpse had also been stabbed some sixty six times and castrated and his cock and balls where nowhere to be found even though it certainly was not the case whatsoever that the police would ever give a shit about looking for them at all and in any case by the time the shattered and bloody and ripped apart and shapeless mess that was the putrid thing that remained of what once had been the sorry bastard and that kind of looked like the T Hyphen One Thousand in Terminator Two Colon Judgment Day the last time it manages to surface and shriek and fling its arms around or what is left of them after the T Hyphen Eight Hundred shots him with a grenade launcher causing him to fall into a vat of molten steel had been noticed that cock and those balls had been for days now in the digestive tract of someone or several someones or even already shat out and part also kept in a freezer somewhere and inside a jar filled with formaldehyde displayed as a trophy or as a memorabilia item as well or who the fuck knows or cares what and the shattered and bloody and ripped apart and shapeless mess that was the putrid thing that remained of what once had been the sorry bastard and that kind of looked like the T Hyphen One Thousand in Terminator Two Colon Judgment Day the last time it manages to surface and shriek and fling its arms around or what is left of them after the T Hyphen Eight Hundred shots him with a grenade launcher causing him to fall into a vat of molten steel was found to have a quite considerable amount of H and Roachies in its system and there were no clothes whatsoever to be found anywhere at all and all that was found with the shattered and bloody and ripped apart and shapeless mess that was the putrid thing that remained of what once had been the sorry bastard and that kind of looked like the T Hyphen One Thousand in Terminator Two Colon Judgment Day the last time it manages to surface and shriek and fling its arms around or what is left of them after the T Hyphen Eight Hundred shots him with a grenade launcher causing him to fall into a vat of molten steel was its skateboard and nevertheless there were really almost no resemblances between this particular case and Paranoid Park due particularly to the specific fact that the skateboard was very quickly ruled out as being the object or one of the objects with which the shattered and bloody and ripped apart and shapeless mess that was the putrid thing that remained of what once had been the sorry bastard and that kind of looked like the T Hyphen One Thousand in Terminator Two Colon Judgment Day the last time it manages to surface and shriek and fling its arms around or what is left of them after the T Hyphen Eight Hundred shots him with a grenade launcher causing him to fall into a vat of molten steel given that it sustained no major damage and there had not been found any blood or tissue or fragments of bones or brains on it and the only legacy the sorry bastard and the shattered and bloody and ripped apart and shapeless mess that was the putrid thing that remained of what once had been the sorry bastard and that kind of looked like the T Hyphen One Thousand in Terminator Two Colon Judgment Day the last time it manages to surface and shriek and fling its arms around or what is left of them after the T Hyphen Eight Hundred shots him with a grenade launcher causing him to fall into a vat of molten steel left behind it was the fact that the whole affair annoyed and frustrated a fair number of people due to the fact that the whole fucking murder or whatever the fuck fucking incident had been a major inconvenience and pain in the ass for everyone including the Police Department because they had to pretend to be investigating the death or murder or whatever the fuck of as they called yet another worthless piece of shit scumbag lowlife whore who no one gave a shit about and also for the people who frequented the building because access was for some time well kind of restricted and limited on account of it being a crime scene or whatever and all but very soon after everything returned to normal when the Police Department officially ruled the thing as death due to Undetermined Causes particularly after a certain woman wearing very fucking high heels and shitloads of Cartier and Tiffany and Bvlgari and Piaget and Harry Winston jewelry every fucking where and whose hair was very straight and had eyes that were very fucking green and it could be seen that she had some kind of tattoo that was like an imitation of the spots of cheetahs showing in her neck and who said her name was Niviva Darkbloom had visited the Police Department and then the shattered and bloody and ripped apart and shapeless mess that was the putrid thing that remained of what once had been the sorry bastard and that kind of looked like the T Hyphen One Thousand in Terminator Two Colon Judgment Day the last time it manages to surface and shriek and fling its arms around or what is left of them after the T Hyphen Eight Hundred shots him with a grenade launcher causing him to fall into a vat of molten steel was quickly cremated and buried who the fuck cares where by the Police Department and many people including Eve and Illona were a teeny tiny tad relieved even though they had never been truly worried because they knew no fucking one would give a shit about doing any fucking thing whatsoever regarding that so called case and they had been actually the ones who had helped arrange the kidnapping with the hostess and others and in fact it had actually been the case that there had been a party which had included even a ridiculous idiot that was blindfolded and was wearing a fucking bow tie and a motherfucking white jacket that actually had embroidered a fucking nightingale on the left side and this ridiculous idiot played an old and quite deteriorated synthesizer at a low volume and at seemingly random intervals and therefore the idiot would play for some five minutes and then stop for like ten fucking minutes and then play for like three minutes and then stop again for like fifteen minutes and anyway it was not like any fucking one was paying the slightest attention to that stupid keyboardist and so this party to which the fourteen year old sorry bastard that would in the very near future end up becoming the putrid thing that remained of what once had been the sorry bastard and that kind of looked like the T Hyphen One Thousand in Terminator Two Colon Judgment Day the last time it manages to surface and shriek and fling its arms around or what is left of them after the T Hyphen Eight Hundred shots him with a grenade launcher causing him to fall into a vat of molten steel even along with his skateboard had been dragged to with lies and the help of Roachies and as soon as he had placed a single foot in the entrance of the place where this party was held he had been beaten the motherfucking shit out of by a very fierce mob of individuals and among them was the very hostess of the party who this particular had ordered everyone to call her and refer to her only as Gloria S and fists and nails and high heels and elbows and male shoes were landing on him every fucking where and without respite and the fourteen year old sorry bastard that would in the very near future end up becoming the putrid thing that remained of what once had been the sorry bastard and that kind of looked like the T Hyphen One Thousand in Terminator Two Colon Judgment Day the last time it manages to surface and shriek and fling its arms around or what is left of them after the T Hyphen Eight Hundred shots him with a grenade launcher causing him to fall into a vat of molten steel was bleeding all over and just crying hysterically and not even being able to speak a single word due to the surprise and the severity of the manhandling and the mob was having the time of their lives laughing and cheering and applauding and then the females started ripping the shreds of clothes still on him off and then he was naked and everybody started pinching and squeezing him all fucking over and he was cuffed behind his back and gagged with a ball gag and shackles were put to his ankles and he was dragged to a cell and so this party had the fourteen year old sorry bastard that would in the very near

future end up becoming the putrid thing that
remained of what once had been the sorry bastard
and that kind of looked like the T Hyphen One
Thousand in Terminator Two Colon Judgment
Day the last time it manages to surface and shriek
and fling its arms around or what is left of them
after the T Hyphen Eight Hundred shots him
with a grenade launcher causing him to fall into a
vat of molten steel installed in that adjoining cell
where there awaited them everything needed for
the fucking piece meal destruction of the fourteen
year old sorry bastard that would in the very near
future end up becoming the putrid thing that
remained of what once had been the sorry bastard
and that kind of looked like the T Hyphen One
Thousand in Terminator Two Colon Judgment
Day the last time it manages to surface and shriek
and fling its arms around or what is left of them
after the T Hyphen Eight Hundred shots him
with a grenade launcher causing him to fall into a
vat of molten steel and his agony had been very
very very slow and it had been quite ghastly all to
the amusement and pleasure of this party of
several individuals and the hostess had torn off a
piece of skin from the neck of the fourteen year
old sorry bastard that would in the very near

future end up becoming the putrid thing that remained of what once had been the sorry bastard and that kind of looked like the T Hyphen One Thousand in Terminator Two Colon Judgment Day the last time it manages to surface and shriek and fling its arms around or what is left of them after the T Hyphen Eight Hundred shots him with a grenade launcher causing him to fall into a vat of molten steel just from a bite and he started bleeding quite a bit from that wound and she delighted herself drinking a very good amount of that blood and then while the fourteen year old sorry bastard that would in the very near future end up becoming the putrid thing that remained of what once had been the sorry bastard and that kind of looked like the T Hyphen One Thousand in Terminator Two Colon Judgment Day the last time it manages to surface and shriek and fling its arms around or what is left of them after the T Hyphen Eight Hundred shots him with a grenade launcher causing him to fall into a vat of molten steel was still alive she had ordered some of her guests to torn off his foreskin with various very sharp knives and those guests had obeyed their hostess and the fourteen year old sorry bastard that would in the very near future end up becoming the putrid thing that remained of what once had been the sorry bastard and that kind of looked like the T Hyphen One Thousand in Terminator Two Colon Judgment Day the last time it manages to surface and shriek and fling its arms around or what is left of them after the T Hyphen Eight Hundred shots him with a grenade launcher causing him to fall into a vat of molten steel had emitted almost inhuman howls of despair and utter pain and everybody now laughed even harder and louder and the hostess snapped her fingers and ordered all her enormous hunting knives be brought to her and a couple of servants obliged and walked quickly to wherever the fuck those enormous fucking hunting knives were and fetched them and quickly brought them to their mistress and they were something like six enormous fucking hunting knives and the hostess proceeded to hand them to some of her guests and ordered them to use them on the fourteen year old sorry bastard that would in the very near future end up becoming the putrid thing that remained of what once had been the sorry bastard and that kind of looked like the T Hyphen One Thousand in Terminator Two Colon Judgment Day the last time it manages to surface and shriek and fling its arms around or what is left of them after the T Hyphen Eight Hundred shots him with a grenade launcher causing him to fall into a vat of molten steel and the guests obeyed and started hacking at and stabbing the fourteen year old sorry bastard that would in the very near future end up becoming the putrid thing that remained of what once had been the sorry bastard and that kind of looked like the T Hyphen One Thousand in Terminator Two Colon Judgment Day the last time it manages to surface and shriek and fling its arms around or what is left of them after the T Hyphen Eight Hundred shots him with a grenade launcher causing him to fall into a vat of molten steel and they were stabbing his legs and running the blades all they way though and they were also doing the same or very similar shit to his arms and his face and his armpits and then they cut off both of the nipples of the fourteen year old sorry bastard that would in the very near future end up becoming the putrid thing that remained of what once had been the sorry bastard and that kind of looked like the T Hyphen One Thousand in Terminator Two Colon Judgment Day the last time it manages to surface and shriek and fling its arms around or what is left of them after the T

Hyphen Eight Hundred shots him with a grenade launcher causing him to fall into a vat of molten steel and that they did it as slowly as possible so that the agony of the fourteen year old sorry bastard that would in the very near future end up becoming the putrid thing that remained of what once had been the sorry bastard and that kind of looked like the T Hyphen One Thousand in Terminator Two Colon Judgment Day the last time it manages to surface and shriek and fling its arms around or what is left of them after the T Hyphen Eight Hundred shots him with a grenade launcher causing him to fall into a vat of molten steel could maybe be prolonged and these guests had no fucking idea if that would indeed be the case and were wondering and pondering and considering and reflecting and philosophizing and balancing pros and cons about the matter but anyway after some seconds and some very loud yells emanating from the lungs and the larynx and the voice box and the esophagus and the throat and the tongue and the mouth of the hostess they just said, fuck it, and they figured it would had to be anyway and so they indeed performed the cutting off or amputation of the two nipples of the fourteen year old sorry bastard that would in the very near future end up becoming the putrid thing that remained of what once had been the sorry bastard and that kind of looked like the T Hyphen One Thousand in Terminator Two Colon Judgment Day the last time it manages to surface and shriek and fling its arms around or what is left of them after the T Hyphen Eight Hundred shots him with a grenade launcher causing him to fall into a vat of molten steel with exquisite slowness and the wailings and cries of the fourteen year old sorry bastard that would in the very near future end up becoming the putrid thing that remained of what once had been the sorry bastard and that kind of looked like the T Hyphen One Thousand in Terminator Two Colon Judgment Day the last time it manages to surface and shriek and fling its arms around or what is left of them after the T Hyphen Eight Hundred shots him with a grenade launcher causing him to fall into a vat of molten steel were such delicate and delightful and cheerful and sweet music to the ears of everyone present with the obvious exception of course of the fourteen year old sorry bastard that would in the very near future end up becoming the putrid thing that remained of what once had been the sorry bastard and that kind of looked like the T Hyphen One Thousand in Terminator Two Colon Judgment Day the last time it manages to surface and shriek and fling its arms around or what is left of them after the T Hyphen Eight Hundred shots him with a grenade launcher causing him to fall into a vat of molten steel and one of the female guests took the nipples as a souvenir and later made pin buttons out of them because she was so industrious and creative and had always been since she was a little adorable girl and then the guests who had the enormous fucking hunting knives in their hands started cutting and creating wounds all over the torso and the abdomen of the fourteen year old sorry bastard that would in the very near future end up becoming the putrid thing that remained of what once had been the sorry bastard and that kind of looked like the T Hyphen One Thousand in Terminator Two Colon Judgment Day the last time it manages to surface and shriek and fling its arms around or what is left of them after the T Hyphen Eight Hundred shots him with a grenade launcher causing him to fall into a vat of molten steel and then they did the same to his back and ass cheeks and briefly penetrated his ass hole with the tip of one of those fucking enormous fucking hunting knives and then the hostess put some blood and little pieces of flesh that had once belonged to the body of the fourteen year old sorry bastard that would in the very near future end up becoming the putrid thing that remained of what once had been the sorry bastard and that kind of looked like the T Hyphen One Thousand in Terminator Two Colon Judgment Day the last time it manages to surface and shriek and fling its arms around or what is left of them after the T Hyphen Eight Hundred shots him with a grenade launcher causing him to fall into a vat of molten steel in her cunt pierced with a Christina piercing adorned with a diamond of thirty six carats and then snapped her fingers and ordered something and immediately after that a couple of male guests brought a dog to her and she had the dog lick all that blood and pieces of flesh off her cunt making the hostess moan in delight and smile and laugh and get her pierced nipples even more erect and of course absolutely everything was being captured on both video and photography and then the hostess snapped her fingers once again and two male guests and one female guest grabbed the dog and masturbated it to get its penis erect and the female guest sucked on it for a while and tried their very best to make it rape the fourteen year old sorry bastard that would in the very near future end up becoming the putrid thing that remained of what once had been the sorry bastard and that kind of looked like the T Hyphen One Thousand in Terminator Two Colon Judgment Day the last time it manages to surface and shriek and fling its arms around or what is left of them after the T Hyphen Eight Hundred shots him with a grenade launcher causing him to fall into a vat of molten steel by inserting the fucking canine cock in the ass hole of the fourteen year old sorry bastard that would in the very near future end up becoming the putrid thing that remained of what once had been the sorry bastard and that kind of looked like the T Hyphen One Thousand in Terminator Two Colon Judgment Day the last time it manages to surface and shriek and fling its arms around or what is left of them after the T Hyphen Eight Hundred shots him with a grenade launcher causing him to fall into a vat of molten steel and succeeded only moderately and somewhat unsatisfyingly for their taste and then one of the male guests used one of the enormous fucking hunting knives to slowly decapitate the dog and the wailings of agony and pain of the dog and the wailings of agony and pain the fourteen year old sorry bastard that would in the very near future end up becoming the putrid thing that remained of what once had been the sorry bastard and that kind of looked like the T Hyphen One Thousand in Terminator Two Colon Judgment Day the last time it manages to surface and shriek and fling its arms around or what is left of them after the T Hyphen Eight Hundred shots him with a grenade launcher causing him to fall into a vat of molten steel suddenly formed a chorus of two very similar voices and tones and it was something that could not be heard even coming form the fucking best boy choir in all of fucking Austria and that made all the party guests laugh out loud and that was too such delicate and delightful and cheerful and sweet music to the ears of all the merry guests and had such a special and particular and truly impressive and delicious atonality and it was certain that not even György fucking Ligeti nor Krzysztof fucking Penderecki could have composed it not even during the biggest and most insane and wildest trip of both acid and H and finally the head of the dog was completely of after that guest finally succeeded in severing every

single piece of fur and flesh and tissue and artery
and vein and trachea and bone from the neck of
the fucking beast and then proceeded to fuck the
asshole of the dead and headless animal to the
encouragement and laughter and cheering of
everyone with the exception of the hostess and
afterwards a couple of other male guests tried
their luck with the asshole of the dead and headless
animal and then the female guest who had sucked
the cock of the fucking beast grabbed one of the
fucking enormous hunting fucking knives and cut
off its penis and started to suck it once again and
afterwards tried to stuck it inside her cunt and
then tried to stuck it inside her ass hole and then a
few other female guests started laughing and took
the bestial cock from the former female guests and
then these other female guests started sucking the
bestial cock and then tried to fuck their cunts and
their ass holes with it and then most of the party
guests proceeded with the destruction and torture
and killing of the fourteen year old sorry bastard
that would in the very near future end up
becoming the putrid thing that remained of what
once had been the sorry bastard and that kind of
looked like the T Hyphen One Thousand in
Terminator Two Colon Judgment Day the last

time it manages to surface and shriek and fling its arms around or what is left of them after the T Hyphen Eight Hundred shots him with a grenade launcher causing him to fall into a vat of molten steel and kept on using those fucking enormous fucking hunting fucking knives and after a while the head of the fourteen year old sorry bastard that would in the very near future end up becoming the putrid thing that remained of what once had been the sorry bastard and that kind of looked like the T Hyphen One Thousand in Terminator Two Colon Judgment Day the last time it manages to surface and shriek and fling its arms around or what is left of them after the T Hyphen Eight Hundred shots him with a grenade launcher causing him to fall into a vat of molten steel was almost off just like a very good part of one of his arms and then someone went away for some seconds and came back with a steel baseball bat and began using it to bash the face and the skull of the fourteen year old sorry bastard that would in the very near future end up becoming the putrid thing that remained of what once had been the sorry bastard and that kind of looked like the T Hyphen One Thousand in Terminator Two Colon Judgment Day the last time it manages to

surface and shriek and fling its arms around or
what is left of them after the T Hyphen Eight
Hundred shots him with a grenade launcher
causing him to fall into a vat of molten steel and
everybody cheered and clapped and laughed when
the nose of the fourteen year old sorry bastard that
would in the very near future end up becoming
the putrid thing that remained of what once had
been the sorry bastard and that kind of looked like
the T Hyphen One Thousand in Terminator Two
Colon Judgment Day the last time it manages to
surface and shriek and fling its arms around or
what is left of them after the T Hyphen Eight
Hundred shots him with a grenade launcher
causing him to fall into a vat of molten steel had
disappeared and when the sounds of the skull
being pulverized and they all began cheering and
clapping and laughing when one of the female
guests took one of the fucking enormous fucking
hunting fucking knives and carved out one of the
eyes of the fourteen year old sorry bastard that
would in the very near future end up becoming
the putrid thing that remained of what once had
been the sorry bastard and that kind of looked like
the T Hyphen One Thousand in Terminator Two
Colon Judgment Day the last time it manages to

surface and shriek and fling its arms around or what is left of them after the T Hyphen Eight Hundred shots him with a grenade launcher causing him to fall into a vat of molten steel if he was not it already and they all looked at what remained of his face and being realistic and in all honesty that fucking thing could not even be considered a face at all anymore and then the hostess finally ordered for the complete removal of the cock and the balls of the fourteen year old sorry bastard and the guests obliged of course and all the while New Order on speakers had been saying, when i was a very small boy very small boys talked to me now that weve grown up together theyre afraid of what they see thats the price that we all pay our valued destiny comes to nothing i cant tell you where were going, and the fourteen year old sorry bastard had bit it muffling pure and absolute agony and then the hostess could not hold it any longer and squirted very very very fucking copiously and afterwards the hostess ordered to be handed the mutilated cock of the fourteen year old sorry bastard and had done her best to penetrate both her cunt and her asshole with it and finally had used it to just masturbate her cunt with and then when she had gotten bored with that she grabbed the scrotum and a knife and used the knife to tear off one testicle and then she put it on her plate and grabbed a fork and a knife and then proceeded to delight herself wit the eating of it slowly and enjoying every single bite and all the while one of the guests had been fucking what was left of the asshole and then every one proceeded to further destroy what was left of the body and eat some parts of it and then some of the male guests at the orders of their hostess had transported the shattered and bloody and ripped apart and shapeless mess that was the putrid thing that remained of what once had been the sorry bastard and that kind of looked like the T Hyphen One Thousand in Terminator Two Colon Judgment Day the last time it manages to surface and shriek and fling its arms around or what is left of them after the T Hyphen Eight Hundred shots him with a grenade launcher causing him to fall into a vat of molten steel from the place where the party had been held to that room of that building where it had been found and they also transported the skateboard and placed it near the shattered and bloody and ripped apart and shapeless mess that was the putrid thing that remained of what once had been the sorry bastard and that kind of

looked like the T Hyphen One Thousand in
Terminator Two Colon Judgment Day the last
time it manages to surface and shriek and fling its
arms around or what is left of them after the T
Hyphen Eight Hundred shots him with a grenade
launcher causing him to fall into a vat of molten
steel and that seemed to them like a nice touch
and that was that, and, anyway, all this
remembrance of the starving artists and especially
of their smoking habits had reminded A how
motherfucking desperately he needed his Black
Devils since it had been like a motherfucking
thousand hours since his last one for fuck's sake,
so he searched desperately for his fucking backpack
because they were inside wondering where the
fuck was it and then fearing the pack might had
been in one of his pockets and maybe the jerk
somehow might had taken it with him because of
how motherfucking imbecilic he was or by
accident or some shit and A wondered why all the
motherfucking jerks had to be so fucking stupid
but would not give up in his search because it
fucking had to be somewhere and it fucking better
be somewhere so he looked inside every single
corner and crevice of his backpack and the pockets
of his hoodie and under the bed and et cetera and

et cetera and fucking et cetera, only to finally sunk into despair which happened to be the despair only a smoker can be familiar with when he knows he definitely lost his last pack or finished the last cigarette and there is no way he can get one more and then it all changed when he went to the bathroom and there behind the toilet he found his last two Black Devils and went to stand in front of the sink and spit into it and open the cold water faucet and rinsed his mouth and spit again and then rinsed his mouth again and then spit again and then grabbed his toothbrush and then placed a very very generous amount of toothpaste on its bristles and started to strongly and frenetically brush his teeth and his tongue and his palate and his gums over and over and over and over again and it was such strong and frenetic the way he was doing it all small amounts of blood appeared and finally rinsed his mouth and spit the foamy and lightly pink water and having done so he took off his hoodie and then his Converse shoes and then his socks and then his t shirt and then his Super Skinny jeans and then his Calvin Klein boxer briefs and immediately produced his lighter and then had to kneel down and grab those two cigarettes and light one and then put it to his small and pink lips and feeling instantly that old familiar relaxing calming disgusting nicotine flavor and that old familiar relief all over his body from head to toe starting in his mouth and his throat after that and then at the same time closed his eyes and leaned his head against the wall and for half a second things seemed almost alright, even his bare ass on top of the cold as fuck floor of the bathroom and for a moment he could consider himself able to finish reading the piece of shit stupid book and writing the subsequent piece of shit stupid paper but anyway he preferred not to think about all that fucking shit that right now as this was his fucking moment enjoying his motherfucking Back Devil and absolutely everything else could go fuck itself for all he gave a shit about and he still had one more left and for a moment which amounted to approximately three seconds he experienced something close to what most human specimens in their fucking idiocy and naivety and ignorance would call contentment or some stupid shit like that and a lost gaze appeared on his face while he was inhaling and exhaling and inhaling and exhaling and inhaling and exhaling and inhaling and exhaling and inhaling and exhaling and inhaling and exhaling and inhaling and

exhaling and inhaling and exhaling and inhaling
and exhaling and inhaling and exhaling and
inhaling and exhaling and inhaling and exhaling
and inhaling and exhaling and inhaling and
exhaling and inhaling and exhaling and inhaling
and exhaling and inhaling and exhaling and
inhaling and exhaling and inhaling and exhaling
and inhaling and exhaling and inhaling and
exhaling and inhaling and exhaling until he
finished the Black Devil which immediately
prompted him to get off his ass and fetch his
lighter and the remaining Black Devil and light it
which caused him to feel again that old relief but
in a much much more tepid way this time
compared to the previous one and as he was once
again inhaling and exhaling and inhaling and
exhaling and inhaling and exhaling and inhaling
and exhaling and inhaling and exhaling and
inhaling and exhaling and inhaling and exhaling
and inhaling and exhaling and inhaling and
exhaling and inhaling and exhaling and inhaling
and exhaling and inhaling and exhaling and
inhaling and exhaling and inhaling and exhaling
and inhaling and exhaling and inhaling and
exhaling and inhaling and exhaling and inhaling
and exhaling and inhaling and exhaling and

inhaling and exhaling and inhaling and exhaling, focused his look on the scars on his wrists and on arms which were now barely visible and then put out the Back Devil on his perfectly hairless left thigh while enjoying the pain and at the same time considering the action a very stupid and idiotic and futile thing to do but as always A saw no fucking point on dwelling on past actions whether they took place six years or ten seconds ago thoughts and yet all that did not stop him from touching and feeling the burn and deep down admiring this latest work of and by and on himself and feeling that very very old desire or impulse or urge or will or whatever the fuck to continue and to start again and to start over and to begin to transform his body into a collection of fucking scars like he had desired and had almost succeeded in doing some five years ago, and a man who wants to mutilate himself is pretty well damned, but instead grabbed the two cigarette butts and opened the toilet lid and threw them into the toilet and closed the lid and flushed and then opened the lid again and arched his back and put three fingers of his right hand on his lips but at the last moment decided not to and put them away and closed the lid back again and went to the tub and opened the faucet and watched as the water ran waiting for it to get hot and the water ran and suddenly steam started to appear and he put the plug on and now waited for the tub to fill and dipped his left arm and waving it inside the now hot as fuck water and waited and waited as the water kept running and running and running and running until the tub was filled and then got off his flat and small and almost non existent ass and got in submerging first his right foot and then his left one with some people perhaps even considering that he was experiencing some sort of enjoyment or something like that due to the sensations that he felt while sinking himself into that hot as fuck water and feeling how his burn stung even much more now and he continued to sink himself until his flat and small and almost non existent ass was seated on the now hot as fuck as well white acrylic and the burn stung and he was now submerged all the way to the neck and the burn stung and then waited a few seconds and then shoved his entire head in and the water soaked his golden hair dark chestnut and he was holding his breath and thinking about how it would be to die by drowning and feeling his body turn weightless and loving that sensation and imagining he was drowning in some far away and secluded and secret lake only he knew about and all of this while of course keeping his eyes wide shut because he had never been able to keep them open under water and he was avoiding as much as humanly possible touching the acrylic with his hands or his arms or his feet or his perfectly hairless legs and was floating almost and still holding his breath trying to put aside so many images and thoughts and memories and shit that were appearing in his mind and feeling how his whole body was twitching due to the lack of oxygen and how his face and his chest and his throat were almost like in a panic begging him for that fucking oxygen and all of this managed to make him forget about the burn and about how it was stinging and after some five seconds he finally let his head out of the water and silently started to pant and gasp and then started breathing through his mouth and nose and feeling his heart beating so fucking fast and feeling as though it was going to pop out of his heaving chest and knew his

whole fucking face was now pink and continued
to shallowly and fastly breathe through his mouth
and his nose and feel his frenetic heartbeat and
strived to thoroughly notice and experience such
sensations and waited until his breathing and his
heartbeat slowly began to normalize themselves
again or something and then closed both of his
eyes and covered his face with both of his hands
and slightly tilted it downwards with both arms
pressed against his flat flat flat chest with the
supremely jutting out ribs and sternum and
collarbones and tried to clear his mind and forget
he existed and forget he was he for just a moment
and it was all in vain of course and then after
finally giving up clenched his fists and pulled his
right arm with the little and thin beaded red
bracelet out of the tub and reached for his Super
Skinnies and from the right front pocket he
produced his black pocket knife and opened it
and pressed the blade against his left wrist where
his small and thin gold Cartier bracelet was and
remembered how he had said, because i deserve it,
when someone had asked him why he had bought
it a couple of days after he had done so and pressed
and pressed until blood started to appear and
dragged the blade for about one inch and then

stopped and folded the pocket knife and threw it across the room and it was a shallow cut and he felt stupid and guilty in part for doing such a thing and in part for making such a shallow cut and submerged his left wrist in the water and now the cut stung as well and he liked it and he hated himself and saw how the blood continued to run in small quantities and then finally grabbed his Fekkai Silky Straight Ironless Shampoo with his left hand and opened it and put a quarter size amount of it on his right palm and then applied it to his hair and began to lather up from roots to ends using vertical strokes and lathered and lathered and then rinsed with so much incredible fucking care and then grabbed his Fekkai Silky Straight Ironless Conditioner with his left hand and put some on his right palm and applied it to his hair with so much incredible fucking care and then grabbed his washcloth with his left hand and his Bleu De Chanel shower gel and applied a greatly generous amount to the washcloth and then put the bottle with the shower gel aside and grabbed the washcloth with his right hand and began washing his naturally one hundred percent hairless face and his nostrils and then his ears and then his neck and then his naturally one hundred percent hairless left arm and then took the washcloth with his left hand and washed his naturally one hundred percent hairless right arm and then grabbed the washcloth with his right hand again and proceeded to wash his naturally one hundred percent hairless armpit and then once again grabbed the washcloth with his left hand and washed his right naturally one hundred percent hairless armpit and afterwards he grabbed the washcloth with his right hand again and then started washing his naturally one hundred percent hairless chest and then his naturally one hundred percent hairless back as much as he could and then his naturally one hundred percent hairless right leg and then its naturally one hundred percent hairless foot and then his naturally one hundred percent hairless left leg followed by its naturally one hundred percent hairless foot and he then washed his naturally one hundred percent hairless buttocks and deep inside his naturally one hundred percent hairless ass crack and after that finally reaching for his completely and absolutely and utterly free of any possible miniscule fucking trace of pubic hair cock and testicles and washing them with great force and roughly scrubbing and scrubbing and scrubbing and scrubbing and scrubbing and scrubbing and scrubbing and scrubbing and scrubbing and scrubbing and scrubbing and scrubbing and scrubbing and scrubbing and scrubbing and scrubbing and scrubbing and scrubbing so much and so hard that he started hurting himself and even squeezed his scrotum and then finally punched it afterwards and then felt the pain all the way to his stomach and he felt the shortness of breath and he felt the slight dizziness and he closed his eyes and arched his back and grabbed the edges of the tub with both hands again breathing fastly and squeezing his eyes and waited and waited and waited and waited and waited and waited until he could move and then finally he rinsed himself from head to toe and lift the plug and looked at how the water was beginning to drain and disappear and he liked seeing that shit and then got up and grabbed one of his immaculately white towels and began drying himself up, first his hair very carefully like he was barely touching it but still delicately massaging it and then his face and then his neck and then his left armpit and then his left arm and then his right armpit and then his right arm and then his chest and then his back and then his flat and small and almost non existent buttocks and his ass crack and then his cock and his scrotum and finally his right leg and then his right foot and then he pulled it outside of the tub and stepped on the floor towel and then he dried his left leg while examining his burn and then his left foot and pulled it outside of the tub as well and placed it on the towel floor as well and when he was finally dry he hung the towel and turned the bathroom lights off and entered the tiny bedroom and turned his bedside lamp on and put a navy blue Calvin Klein boxer briefs on and thought of how many selfies he had taken like this and then posted on his Instagram and on his Tumblr and thought of how the time for selfies and his Tumblr was fucking over and done with and almost too far away and pressed his right hand on his face and sighed and clenched his right fist and thought fuck it and undid his bed and crawled into it and closed his eyes and the anxiety was somewhat high at the moment and he tried to empty his mind and after some ten minutes he fell asleep, though obviously not as deeply at all as when he was given Roachies and he was lying there breathing and not moving at all and he was sleeping and breathing and sleeping and breathing and sleeping and breathing and then suddenly he turned around with his boxer briefs tightly pressed against and barely covering his flat and small and almost non existent ass and he began to breathe a little faster and turned around again into the position he was at the beginning when he first had fallen asleep and he was there with his smooth and straight blond hair and his small and thin and pink lips and his pale skin that clung and was adhered to his skeleton and he was lying there and he slept and then woke up and it was a few minutes past six and he was short of breath and shaking and damp with sweat and pressed his hands against his face and on his Spotify The Cardigans were saying, what did you hear me say yes i said its fine before but i dont think so no more i said its fine before ive changed my mind i take it back, and Eve and

Illona were calling again and he walked towards
his MacBook Pro and sat down in front of it and
answered and there they were Eve and Illona and
they were in bed surrounded by their cats and
their dogs and they were naked at least from the
waist up and they were smiling and smoking and
they were high and hangover or maybe drunk and
Eve was petting and squeezing Illona's left tit and
Illona's hair was now green and was shaven at the
sides and she was wearing purple rimmed glasses
and they started talking, hey new york bitch hows
it going, and A just waved and nodded and they
said, youre quiet slut what have you been up to,
and A did not know what the fuck to say and they
continued, cat got your tongue bitch, and Illona
put hers inside Eve's mouth and said to her, maybe
the little whore bitch wont talk cause shes got a
mouthful of cum, and they both started to laugh
out loud and hysterically and A kinda just stared
at the screen for various seconds and Eve and
Illona looked and smiled at each other like
partners in crime and just said, well goodbye you
sexy little bitch slut, and hung up and on his
iTunes Sleigh Bells were saying, hang me high
theyre gonna bury you theyre gonna finish theyre
gonna stand em up six by six by six you pull the

hood back i wanna know, and A's hands were sweating and he had shortness of breath and he knew the fucking book was lying there but refused to fucking look at it or even acknowledge its fucking existence and he remained there seated on the chair with his hands between his spread legs not knowing where to look or what to do or even what to fucking think and sighing and brought his right hand to his face and covered his mouth and pressed his eyes for a moment and hated himself and then his mind went back to where had he been almost seven hours ago and it was at this fucking club and he did not know what the fuck he was doing there and he never did and there were a lot of hot guys below twenty five but the reality and the truth were that he could not have cared less and those lots of hot guys below twenty five were about half the people there with the other half being old and fat jerks and there were these couple of dudes always whispering at each other's ears and almost always together and one was around twenty and had the body of a thin but strong jock and was shirtless and the other was a fat and bearded jerk somewhere around his late fifties and the jock was dancing and making out with every single dude out there of every age but always looking at the fat and bearded jerk somewhere around his late fifties as if looking for his approval or something and the fat and bearded jerk somewhere around his fifties always limited himself to look back at the jock and smile and rub his cock and his balls through his jeans and A was just looking and he wanted to leave but for some reason he did not and he looked around and suddenly the fat and bearded jerk somewhere around his late fifties was standing next to him, and it was way too fucking close to him for A's taste and A flinched and the jerk just smiled and said, hi, and put his left arm around A's shoulders and told him, hey cutie do you mind giving me a moment of your time here i got some x you want some, and A just shook his head and the jerk led him to a corner away from the crowd and told him, you know youre the most beautiful boy ive ever seen, and A almost threw up and he thought of how he had fucking heard that fucking phrase or some variation of it literally so many motherfucking hundreds of fucking times in his life but did not do nor say shit at all and the jerk leaned in and whispered to his ear and his breath absolutely reeked of stale beer and old imbecile's saliva among many other things and A did not reply and the jerk said to him, come on come on i will make it worth your while i promise you sexy little bitch you fucking little tease i promise you wont regret it here i have lots of dough how old are you are you fifteen or maybe fourteen, and then the jock joined them and he was indeed very attractive and young looking and he just stared at A and the jerk and did not open his mouth at all and A barely nodded and as soon as he had said that the jerk stooped immediately almost kneeling down and undid the button and fly of A's Super Skinnies and got his cock out of his boxer briefs and said, this is fucking beautiful and completely smooth not a single hair i fucking love this i fucking love little slut bitches like you top of the line sluts like you and with all that hair gone you could be fucking nine except your cock would be too fucking big for a nine year old little slut, and then laughed like a demented fucking idiot and then he began fucking drooling like the fucking idiot A was now effectively confirming he was even though in his mind he had been fucking sure as fuck since the very first fucking second and then began sucking A's cock and the jock pulled his cock out and started jerking it with his right hand and rubbing and pinching his nipples with his left hand and moaning like a fucking bitch in heat and the jerk was sucking and sucking and sucking and sucking and suddenly stopped and looked up at A's face and asked him, why arent you hard you sexy little pretty bitch, and immediately afterwards continued on sucking and sucking and sucking and A did not know if the jerk just knew he just would not answer or if he just was not expecting or did not care at all for an answer and the jock was still jerking his cock and rubbing and pinching his nipples and moaning looking at A and at his cock being swallowed over and over and over by the jerk and making sure A was looking at him and how he was jerking his cock and the jerk continued to suck A's completely limp cock and was sucking and sucking and sucking and sucking and sucking and sucking A's cock and ball sack and the front of his boxer briefs and Super Skinnies were now drenched in fucking disgusting spit and phlegm of fucking fat and bearded and motherfucking idiot as fuck jerk somewhere around his late fifties and A just wanted to fucking throw the fuck up right then and there but just did not do it and his cock was still limp as fuck and he wanted to get the fuck out of there and he wanted to throw up and he hated himself but tried as hard as fucking possible to look at the bright side and think about the motherfucking dough to calm himself down and be aware of something remotely resembling some kind of what most people call purpose and the jerk kept on sucking and sucking and sucking and sucking and sucking and fucking sucking and the idiot jock continued on jerking off and A just leaned against the wall with an empty look on his eyes and he rarely moved and the sucking continued and the jerk had a heavy breathing and the jock kept on moaning and the spit kept on flowing and the jerk seemed as though he was having the time of his sad and pathetic and stupid and worthless and wretched and miserable life and A did not even dare to look at the jock's direction or much, much less down and the jerk finally finished and told A, youre so gorgeous, and handed A a crumpled and filthy and sweat-drenched wad of bills and told him, thank you too bad you couldnt get hard boy whats wrong with you little bitch, and A grabbed the wad of bills and put it in his right front pocket and put his limp cock and his balls back inside his boxer briefs and zipped his Supper Skinny jeans' zipper and did his button and got the fuck away from there as quick as he could pretending as though the fucking fat and bearded and fucking idiot as fuck jerk somewhere around his late fifties and the idiot jock weren't there or did not even exist at all and went outside into the cold cold night and counted the cash and there were five one hundred dollar bills and one twenty dollar bill and after counting them A put them back inside his right front pocket and kept on walking and walking and walking and walking and walking and walking towards his apartment trying not to think about anything or at least not about what had just happened and he clenched his fists and began panting and he hated himself but turned his thoughts back at the money to try to calm himself down and kept on walking and walking and walking and walking and walking and walking and walking and walking and walking under the lamp posts and he walked and he walked and he walked and he walked until he reached his building and opened the door and climbed the stairs up and walked until he got to his door and produced his key and got in and turned the lights on got the money out and went towards his tiny bedroom and squatted next to the bed and from under it he got the black box out and opened it and put the money inside and closed it and put it under the bed again and got up and got out of the tiny bedroom and sat on his chair in front of the table and opened and turned his MacBook Pro on and looked to his left and then he saw the motherfucking book and remembered all about it like the motherfucking paper and all that stupid fucking shit and said, fuck fuck fuck fuck fuck fuck, quietly and covered his face with his right hand and slouched in the chair and opened his Spotify and Fiona Apple was then saying, as it came down near so did a weary tear i thought it was a bird but it was just a paper bag, and he opened the book and thought, lets see what the fuck does fucking john fucking j fucking mearsheimer have to say, and now Fiona Apple was saying, and i went crazy again today, and he resumed his reading and finished reading the whole sixty fifth page and closed the book and threw it to the right side of the table and sighed and he was not able to breathe well enough and covered his face with both of his hands and put his elbows against his knees and pulled on his bangs with his fingers and then rubbed his face with his hands ending on his mouth and he left his lower lip pouting and looked away and then approached the keyboard of his MacBook again and began looking at a whole fucking lot of Tumblr blogs and then closed them and then closed his MacBook Pro and then grabbed his iPhone and began looking at a whole fucking lot of Instagram accounts and posts and then he put his iPhone away again and took his MacBook Pro again and opened it began looking at photograph and design sites and blogs and then grabbed the fucking book again and started reading the sixty sixth page and read and fucking read and he was still there hours later still on that chair but now only in his boxer briefs and on his Spotify Perfume Genius was saying, guinea pig hair in a twisted mouth through a hole to the railway and brians face down keep your wits he will not be missed he didnt have a family to begin with, and now was almost seven in the morning and he took a look again at all his scars and touched some of them and rubbed them and his mind wandered again and now went back some eighteen months ago at that night and that thing and he still remembered how things had been for three months prior to everything fucking ending and it all had started that motherfucking night being shit faced as fuck at the old miserable tiny and crummy apartment Graham lived in and he had a lousy Marlboro on and Graham was one of the starving artists who sold their worthless shit on the streets A used to hang out with and it was somewhere around two thirty am and they had been to an art show and it had been execrable of course and they both knew it very well including Graham but A for some reason, maybe to fuck with Graham, had insisted on staying until the worthless thing was over and now Graham was almost unconscious and A was taking advantage of that and doing the piece of shit blow that Graham had bought and was disappointed and annoyed at how fucking bad the fucking blow was but thought what the fuck bad blows better than no blow at all, somethin better than nothin, and it was really bad and it was such a small portion and he was doing the last line exactly when there was a knock on the door and suddenly Graham regained at least some of what passed for consciousness for him and looked around and seemed startled and confused and very surprised and said, what the fuck, and A said, someone is knocking at the door, and Graham said, what, and looked around again and A said again, someone is knocking at the door, and Graham looked at him and A said, someone is knocking at the door, and Graham said, oh right yeah the door yeah right yeah, and they knocked again and Graham said, right oh right yeah, and got up and walked towards the door and opened it and there was a guy around A's age and he had green eyes and messy shoulder length hazelnut hair and was quite thin and medium height and was wearing torn apart Calvin Klein Skinny jeans with more holes on them than A could possibly count and a Givenchy light grey t shirt and he was very hot and handsome and cute and therefore worthy of A's acknowledgement of his existence and maybe even attention and suddenly A became aware that the guy had caused his cock to go hard as fuck and also became aware of the fact that the guy reminded him of one specific porn actor he had a thing for and then the guy said, hey, to Graham and Graham said, hey man, and before he could say, come on in, the guy came in and looked at A for the first time and sort of smiled and Graham took some time to figure out the guy had actually already came in and said, oh, and nodded

and closed the door and looked at the guy and
then at A and said, oh right, and pointed to the
guy and said to A, this is my dipshit idiot cousin
Sean, and then looked at Sean and told him A's
name and A didn't know what to do and
awkwardly got up and then catching A off guard
Sean offered his hand and said, hey man, and A
took the hand and shook it and said, hey, and
Sean smiled and quickly and delicately and almost
unnoticeably licked his lower lip and he and A sat
down and Graham offered him a beer and he
accepted it and then Graham joined Sean and A
with the beer and Sean took the bottle to his lips
and gulped down half the content in an instant
and then looked at A and smiled again and
Graham was unconscious again and Sean said to
A, so how long have you known graham, and A
replied, for a while, and Sean nodded and asked
A, so how old are you, and A said, sixteen you, and
Sean replied, eighteen, and then said, so what do
you do, and A replied i go to high school how
about you, and Sean said, nothing much at the
moment ive been painting and taking a few
photographs until i decide whether i want to go to
college or not, and A said, cool, and then
immediately started talking about the thing he

liked the most in this piece of shit world, after vodka and maybe, just maybe cigarettes and maybe his clothes, of course and that was photography and taking photographs and Sean said, so you take photographs too really, and A said, yeah, and Sean said, cool tell me about it, and A started talking about his photography and about his Tumblr blog and about his Instagram account and about all his cameras, some of them he had had since he was six years old and A talked about how he had started at six with his Polaroid S X Hyphen Seventy and how he still had it and why he loved it even though it was an inferior camera and how he thought he was cool and how annoying he found the fact that so many idiots now were buying that model again and using it and how he thought they were all fucking idiots who knew nothing about photography and then he talked about how at eight years old or so he started using the Nikon F E and all he had learned with it and then how he had moved year or so later from the Nikon F E to the Nikon F Two and how he appreciated the differences and the new challenges and how much fun he had had with it and then he talked about how at eleven years or so he had bought his Canon A Two Slash A Two E and how he had loved it and how cool he had thought it was back then and how it had helped his photography to grow and mature and they talked and talked and talked for around forty minutes and then they headed for the bedroom and closed the door and Sean said, so youve been taking photographs for almost ten years now, and A replied, yes, and before he could add anything Sean had his tongue inside A's mouth and they kissed and Sean's tongue was very deep inside A's mouth and reached and reached and it momentarily rubbed A's palate and then it went outside and gently licked A's lips and then A stuck out his tongue and introduced it in Sean's mouth and Sean put his hands on each of A's shoulders and once again introduced his tongue inside A's mouth and his hands reached further and he put all his fingers on the back of A's neck and then he dragged them down across A's chest and stomach and then he reached A's crotch and felt his hard cock and his balls and rubbed them and then he took his right hand went up A's ass-crack through his Super Skinnies and then he grabbed the bottom of A's t shirt and pulled it up and took it off and kissed A's neck and put his hands on A's arms and then dragged them to his chest and rubbed his tiny and flat and pale pink nipples and then undid A's Super Skinnies' button and zipper and led him to the bed and laid him down face up and slid down the Super Skinnies and rubbed his face on A's crotch and then took those off as well freeing A's hard cock and began sucking on it and then on his balls and then took his shirt off and got rid of A's Converses and socks as well as his own and then undid his jeans and slid them off and did the same with his boxers and he was very hard and uncut and he got on the bed on top of A and they kissed and then Sean continued kissing and biting A's neck and opened A's legs apart and A bended his knees and Sean spit on his hand and spread his spit across his cock and introduced it in A's asshole and they fucked and fucked and fucked for a long time and hours later A woke up and his head was on Sean's chest and Sean had his arms around him and A's right arm was across Sean's stomach and then Sean woke up and looked down and smiled and said, hey gorgeous, and they kissed and after that they remained in the same position on top of the bed until A got up and began getting dressed and Sean did the same and they left Graham's apartment as he was still passed the fuck out on the couch and they got out to the street by the hand and walked and walked and walked and walked and walked and walked and talked and talked and talked and talked and talked and talked and it was like eight in the morning and they continued walking and talking and talking and walking and walking and talking and talking and walking and walking and talking until they got to the house where A slept some nights and kept his stuff at and they said their goodbyes and Sean kissed A and said, see you later cutie, and A replied, later, and went inside and all through the whole fucking day they kept on texting and neither of them got apart from their iPhones for a fucking minute and for the next three months they spent as much time together as possible every single day and Sean went with A to all the piece-of-shit art galleries and exhibitions and shows at one am A always wanted to go without fucking complaining fucking once and sometimes he would even say hi to and shake hands with the piece of shit and pedantic fag so fucking called artist and tell him, congratulations your works cool its quite unique, and A posted a selfie on his Tumblr blog and on his Instagram account holding a handwritten sign all in caps that covered his mouth saying, now love is all ive got, accompanied by a heart that read inside it, a plus s, and a four second video where he said, i love you, and then kissed the camera and that was practically everything he posted on his Tumblr account for those three months and back then he loved having Sean's cock inside his asshole fucking it and even stopped seeing any of the jerks even though he missed the money and with the exception of the Roachies, all the substances that they used to give him like fuck until one day while he was at the place of one of the guys that he used to fuck and that used to fuck him, Sean sent A a Snapchat text that read, hey look i guess i think its time to stop this i guess goodbye, and that was fucking that and that night A drank shitloads of Grey Goose and Bloom and Johnnie Walker Blue Label and José Cuervo and Absolut One Hundred and wanted to die and when he woke up the next day he messaged back some of the jerks that had been messaging all that time asking him what the fuck was up and where the fuck he was and asking him for dates and even calling up Eve and Illona demanding answers and posted a gif on his Tumblr blog and on his Instagram account that featured some stupid bitch in some kind of movie or TV show drinking vodka and that read, will i get over it no but life goes on, and after that stopped posting at all on his Tumblr blog and on his Instagram account for around a month or so and drank fucktons of Grey Goose and Bloom and Johnnie Walker Blue Label and José Cuervo and Absolut One Hundred every single night and went on all the dates every single jerk and bitch propositioned him and let them do anything and everything they fucking wanted to do with and to him and he was given so many Roachies all the fucking time and so many times he did not even know what was it that the jerk or bitch in question had done to or with him and simply used to wake up all sore and with pain and many times blood everywhere and he did not give a single shit and hoarded all the motherfucking money and around that time he used to sometimes smoke five packs a day and then one day he came back to his Tumblr blog and to his Instagram account and started posting selfies again for a while most of them being semi nude or shirtless ones and sometimes showing off his almost nonexistent ass after which everybody seemed to lust so fucking ridiculously and on Tumblr and on Instagram all the anonymous and non anonymous offerings and horny messages started pouring in again with everybody saying how much they had missed him and how fucking hot he was and what a scrumptious ass he had and he also got a few requests for samples of his cum and bottles filled with his piss and for dirty diapers so everything was seemingly back to fucking normal again and he had decided to fucking escape for good to fucking New York City and now here he was in fucking New York City over a year later remembering all that shit and The Cardigans on his Spotify were saying, you rip me up you spread me all round in the dust of the deed of time and this is not a case of lust you see its not a matter of you versus me its fine the way you want me on your own but in the end its always me alone, and he looked over to the fucking book and grabbed it and stared at the thing and thought, fuck it what the fucking fuck do i fucking care about the tragedy of great power politics fuck you john j mearsheimer fuck it, and threw it across the room and sat there for a moment without moving and then started typing and typing and typing and typing and typing and typing and typing and typing and typing and typing and typing and typing and typing and typing and typing and typing and typing and typing and typing and

typing and typing and typing and typing and
typing and typing and typing and typing and
typing and typing and typing and typing and
typing and typing and typing and typing and
typing and typing and typing and typing and
typing and typing and typing and typing and
typing and typing and typing and typing and
typing and typing and typing and typing and
typing and typing and typing and typing and
typing and typing and typing and typing and
typing and typing and typing and typing and
typing and typing and typing and typing and
typing and typing and typing and typing and
typing and typing and typing and typing and
typing and typing and typing and typing and
typing and typing and typing and typing and
typing and typing and typing and typing and
typing and typing and typing and typing and
typing and typing and typing and typing and
typing and all the shit that he typed had of course
nothing to do with The Tragedy Of Great Power
Politics by John J Mearsheimer and most surely it
said something like how all work and no play
makes A a dull boy all work and no play makes A
a dull boy all work and no play makes A a dull boy
all work and no play makes A a dull boy all work

and no play makes A a dull boy all work and no
play makes A a dull boy all work and no play
makes A a dull boy all work and no play makes A
a dull boy all work and no play makes A a dull boy
all work and no play makes A a dull boy all work
and no play makes A a dull boy all work and no
play makes A a dull boy all work and no play
makes A a dull boy all work and no play makes A
a dull boy all work and no play makes A a dull boy
all work and no play makes A a dull boy all work
and no play makes A a dull boy all work and no
play makes A a dull boy all work and no play
makes A a dull boy all work and no play makes A
a dull boy all work and no play makes A a dull boy
all work and no play makes A a dull boy all work
and no play makes A a dull boy all work and no
play makes A a dull boy all work and no play
makes A a dull boy all work and no play makes A
a dull boy all work and no play makes A a dull boy
all work and no play makes A a dull boy all work
and no play makes A a dull boy all work and no
play makes A a dull boy all work and no play
makes A a dull boy all work and no play makes A
a dull boy all work and no play makes A a dull boy
all work and no play makes A a dull boy all work
and no play makes A a dull boy all work and no

play makes A a dull boy all work and no play
makes A a dull boy all work and no play makes A
a dull boy all work and no play makes A a dull boy
all work and no play makes A a dull boy all work
and no play makes A a dull boy all work and no
play makes A a dull boy all work and no play
makes A a dull boy all work and no play makes A
a dull boy all work and no play makes A a dull boy
all work and no play makes A a dull boy all work
and no play makes A a dull boy all work and no
play makes A a dull boy all work and no play
makes A a dull boy all work and no play makes A
a dull boy all work and no play makes A a dull boy
all work and no play makes A a dull boy all work
and no play makes A a dull boy all work and no
play makes A a dull boy all work and no play
makes A a dull boy all work and no play makes A
a dull boy all work and no play makes A a dull boy
all work and no play makes A a dull boy all work
and no play makes A a dull boy all work and no
play makes A a dull boy all work and no play
makes A a dull boy all work and no play makes A
a dull boy all work and no play makes A a dull boy
all work and no play makes A a dull boy all work
and no play makes A a dull boy all work and no
play makes A a dull boy all work and no play

makes A a dull boy all work and no play makes A
a dull boy all work and no play makes A a dull boy
all work and no play makes A a dull boy all work
and no play makes A a dull boy all work and no
play makes A a dull boy all work and no play
makes A a dull boy all work and no play makes A
a dull boy all work and no play makes A a dull boy
all work and no play makes A a dull boy all work
and no play makes A a dull boy all work and no
play makes A a dull boy all work and no play
makes A a dull boy all work and no play makes A
a dull boy all work and no play makes A a dull boy
all work and no play makes A a dull boy all work
and no play makes A a dull boy all work and no
play makes A a dull boy all work and no play
makes A a dull boy all work and no play makes A
a dull boy all work and no play makes A a dull boy
all work and no play makes A a dull boy all work
and no play makes A a dull boy all work and no
play makes A a dull boy all work and no play
makes A a dull boy all work and no play makes A
a dull boy all work and no play makes A a dull boy
all work and no play makes A a dull boy all work
and no play makes A a dull boy all work and no
play makes A a dull boy all work and no play
makes A a dull boy all work and no play makes A

a dull boy all work and no play makes A a dull boy

all work and no play makes A a dull boy all work
and no play makes A a dull boy all work and no
play makes A a dull boy all work and no play
makes A a dull boy all work and no play makes A
a dull boy all work and no play makes A a dull boy
all work and no play makes A a dull boy all work
and no play makes A a dull boy all work and no
play makes A a dull boy all work and no play
makes A a dull boy all work and no play makes A
a dull boy all work and no play makes A a dull boy
all work and no play makes A a dull boy all work
and no play makes A a dull boy all work and no
play makes A a dull boy all work and no play
makes A a dull boy all work and no play makes A
a dull boy all work and no play makes A a dull boy
all work and no play makes A a dull boy all work
and no play makes A a dull boy all work and no
play makes A a dull boy all work and no play
makes A a dull boy all work and no play makes A
a dull boy all work and no play makes A a dull boy
all work and no play makes A a dull boy all work
and no play makes A a dull boy all work and no
play makes A a dull boy all work and no play
makes A a dull boy all work and no play makes A
a dull boy all work and no play makes A a dull boy
all work and no play makes A a dull boy all work

and no play makes A a dull boy all work and no play makes A a dull boy and then remembered he had made an appointment with a loser fan of his from his Tumblr blog and from his Instagram account to see him at a café in the Village at two and thought about standing him up and that made him kind of smile a little and then he finally got up and went to the bedroom and put on a pair of Super Skinnies and socks and a Saint Laurent t shirt and an American Eagle hoodie and a pair of Converse and grabbed his back pack and the craving and the need for Black Devils were overpowering him again and he took his iPhone and his earphones and put them in his pocket and The Cardigans were now saying, my heart is black and my body is blue, and grabbed his keys and closed his MacBook Pro and opened the door of his tiny apartment and then stepped outside and then closed it and then went down the stairs and went outside of the building and started walking and walking and walking and walking and walking and walking and then and there for some reason he started thinking about when he had first met Eve and Illona and it had been six years ago and it had been at a party at their place to which Carrie had taken him because Eve was one of the many cousins of Carrie and it was very crowded and Carrie had introduced him to Eve and Illona and he was quite drunk and they had smiled so fucking big and looked at each other when they met and then he and Eve and Illona started talking and it went on and on and on and on and on and fucking on and when A realized and looked around Carrie had already left and was not among the shitloads of people at the apartment anymore and they told him they had met at Iowa State some five years prior and the complete truth was that it had happened after Eve accused of rape a poor idiot who had never even spoken to her or even really remembered who the fuck she was and she made a mattress in the form of a cock and balls although in reality she had emotionally manipulated some stupid dudes to make it for her and she took to walking around all over campus dragging that cock and balls shaped mattress with her everywhere and of course she attracted a lot of attention with a lot of people calling her brave and empowered and she received a fair amount of journalistic and academic and critical coverage and praise and she kept on walking around all over campus dragging that cock and balls shaped mattress with her everywhere and she was named Victim Of The Year or some bullshit like that by certain groups and by certain art magazine and that was when Illona became aware of the new celebrity on campus and decided she wanted some attention as well so she also accused the same poor idiot of rape although they had never crossed paths or been in the same place at the same time ever or looked at or noticed each other at fucking all and over time the poor idiot killed himself or something and Eve and Illona decided they wanted each other and soon enough they were

making shitloads of money dealing blow and H
and that was after Eve finally stopped dragging
that cock and balls shaped mattress fucking
everywhere because it was not white anymore on
account of being so dirty on account of Eve
dragging the fucking thing all fucking around all
the fucking time and now the thing was all brown
and Eve decided to end his crusade because she
did not want to have her reputation tarnished and
have all the pity and support she had received
taken from her over some stupid fucking
accusation of racism or some other idiotic shit like
that and that was the happy happy happy and
great and lovely and charming and beautiful and
warming and endearing and sweet and and fairy
tale love story of Eve and Illona and they were
now living together and they were holding hands
all the time and had just started in a new business
venture and there were lots of people of A's age
and high school age and they told him they liked
him a lot and invited him to another party they
were having at their place again two weeks after
that and A had said, cool yeah sure ok, and after
some more vodka and another cigarette and some
more pills he had gone back home and two weeks
after he was at Eve and Illona's place again for the

party except this time Carrie was nowhere to be seen at all and this time the apartment was crowded again except now almost everybody was from college age up and there was this big and ripped and tall and kind of hot or so A thought, frat jock checking him out and Eve and Illona were so glad to see A and immediately gave him something to drink and an Absolut Apple jelly shot and after he had finished the drink they immediately gave him another one and they started to talk and the frat jock was still looking at him and staring and was also occasionally looking at Eve and Illona and smiling at them and they were always smiling back at him and A finished yet another drink and either Eve or Illona went immediately for one more drink for him and both Eve and Illona were urging him all the fucking time to finish his drinks as fast as possible over and over and over and over and over and fucking over again and suddenly A was feeling very tired and weary and dizzy and confused and weak and Eve and Illona were laughing out loud having so much fun and insisted A stayed and kept on drinking and gave him another drink and a cigarette and then they went to talk to someone else and the frat jock approached A and the frat jock was wearing very fine clothes and a Rolex that looked brand new and he started talking to A and introduced himself and his name was Mike and he was smiling and then looked at Eve and Illona who looked back at him and he smiled at them and they smiled back at him and A was seeing it all but was completely confused and fucked up and Mike continued to talk to A and he talked and talked and talked and talked and talked and talked for what seemed like a fucking eternity and A was so confused and did not fucking know what the fuck was up and certainly was not paying attention to this inebriated and coked up as fuck Mike entity at all and could barely stand up and then Mike kissed him and put his arms around him and grabbed his right hand and led him to a room and closed the door and there he took all of the clothes A had on him off and made him lay on the bed and slapped him and told him, you like big studs like me dont you you little fag slut, and smiled and laughed and said, what a cute little dick you got, and then unbuttoned and unzipped his pants and slipped his cock from his boxers and then fingered his asshole with his index finger and his middle finger and his fucking ring finger and then proceeded to open A's legs so wide A thought they were going to break or some shit but anyway it was all happening in a very strong daze and then Mike made him bend his knees up until they were pressed against his upper body and then Mike spread those flat and small and almost non existent buttocks of A very fucking wide to take a very good fucking look at his small and pink and unpolluted and pristine and absolutely hairless asshole and then began laughing out loud and then said with a huge grin on his face, how cute we got a virgin here, and smiled so fucking wide and then said, lets take your cherry gorgeous princess, and then fucked A several times for an entire fucking hour and no matter how immensely A turned him on he was under such an enormous influence of substances after each fucking time he came it took him a while to get his cock rock fucking hard again and all throughout that fucking hour he kept on blabbering on and on and on and on and on and fucking on about how much he loved taking the cherries of cute and skinny twinks and how A was the cutest twink he had ever had and it hurt a fucking lot and the barely conscious A just wished that inebriated and coked up as fuck Mike entity would just fucking shut his cunting trap already even for just a fucking millisecond and stop hurting and slapping him so bad and get the motherfucking thing whatever it was over with already and then Mike came or whatever and then left and A completely lost whatever tiny amount of consciousness he was still clinging to and five hours later or so he woke up and all the noise from the party had ceased and his asshole hurt and burned like a motherfucker and he had cum all over it and some blood and he felt still more cum inside of him and then he got up and was barely able to do so at all but still did it and he had a motherfucking headache like a pillow and he was still somewhat dizzy and put his clothes on and went outside of the room and now there were only Eve and Illona in the apartment and they were sitting at the table talking and talking and talking very softly and would not shut the fuck up and occasionally laughing and smiling all the time and they were getting baked and when they heard and saw him they immediately and finally shut the fuck up and kept on smiling and A said, hi good morning i mean good afternoon i think I mean i guess i, and then both Eve and Illona burst out laughing out loud like fucking coked up idiots and A waved at them and said, uh i think im gonna go now i guess so uh bye i guess, and then Eve said, wait, and got up and gave him ten one hundred bucks bills and told him, your cut gorgeous, and A just looked at her for a moment and for some reason for a very brief instant the image of a new born fucking baby coming out of the cunt of his mother and not crying or screaming at all but smiling very broadly showing a full set of very sharp teeth came to his mind and then immediately he forced his own mind to return to where he actually was and then said, uh so uh i uh ok, not really fully grasping yet exactly what the fuck was going on there then and Illona said, he might like to see you again, and winked and smiled and Eve smiled and A just got out of there and he could barely walk due to the fact that his fucking asshole hurt so motherfucking much but still he was fucking exhilarated and almost hyperventilating and worrying he might had been hallucinating due to those fucking ten one hundred bucks bills in his fucking pocket and he could not believe that at all and he could not believe that he had one thousand dollars on his fucking power and they were just and only for him to do whatever the fuck he wanted with them and he had got them without having to do any work but just letting that inebriated and coked up as

fuck Mike entity who was also idiotic and retarded
and and violent and closeted and fucking ripped
and tall and handsome drug him and do whatever
the fuck he had wanted to him and with him and
to his body and with his body but A immediately
put those thoughts out of mind and put them in a
secret drawer inside his brain and that drawer had
a key and he used to lock that drawer and maybe
the key got lost or maybe it did not or maybe it
would get lost someday or maybe it would not
and A though, fuck it, and, whatever, and that was
that and three weeks later Eve and Illona arranged
a date for him and when he arrived to the place for
which they had gave him all the directions it was a
massive and monstrous and mostly white and
seemingly very new Mc Mansion and there were a
Land Rover and two Mercedes Benz and a Porsche
parked outside and A rang the door and a jerk
somewhere around his thirties opened and as
soon as he saw A he smiled like he was Daniel
fucking Plainview and had just found a whole
fucking ocean of motherfucking oil beneath his
feet and no one could get at it except for him or as
if he was The fucking Wolf of fucking Wall
fucking Street and had just embezzled a fucking
idiot of twenty fucking five fucking million

fucking dollars and A asked if this was the S Family residence and the jerk replied, of course, and said, come on in, and A went inside and the jerk introduced himself as Jack and he and A shook hands and Jack was wearing a gold watch and a gold wedding ring and a red jacket and led him to a huge living room and as soon as A entered the living room Jack turned the sound system off which was playing Baby Did A Bad Bad Thing by Chris Isaak and told A to sit down and so A sat down and then Jack offered A a drink and A said, ok sure, and just then a woman of approximately the same age as Jack entered and she was wearing a very capacious and loose fitting grey dress and black shoes with very fucking high heels and shitloads of Cartier and Tiffany and Bvlgari and Piaget and Harry fucking Winston jewelry every fucking where and her hair was very straight and he had eyes that were very fucking green and it could be seen that she had some kind of tattoo that was like an imitation of the spots of cheetahs showing in her neck and then the woman introduced herself to A as V and sat next to him and stared at him and finally said, i cant fucking believe this one is even prettier than in the pics those crazy dyke bitches sent, and then added, fucking unbelievable, and then ran the fingers with long as fuck and painted black nails of her left hand along a strand of the hair on the head of A and then grinned and then pulled on the strand of A's hair and held it and then finally released it and A didn't move and then V said, too bad marc isnt here to see and check out and enjoy this little bitch, and Jack said while pouring the drink he was about to give A, hey i dont thi, and V said, shut the fuck up fucking faggot, and then continued, i bet steve would be happy knowing this little bitch is of his propriety its been such a long long time since weve seen him, and Jack said very alarmed, really you shouldnt keep mentio, and V said, shut the fuck up fucking faggot, and then went on to say how A was a great propriety of The Corporation and Jack again opened his fucking mouth and said in a very low voice, ssshhh please enough alrea, and V replied to him, shut the fuck up fucking faggot, and then she went on saying they should go to d c again soon and that it had been so long since they had been down there and Jack said, really, and V snapped, shut the fuck up fucking faggot, and after a little while Jack came back with a glass and gave it to A and it was supposed to be a glass of fucking Elit or some shit and it seemed so fucking strange and smelled kind of funny and bad and A drank and V put her arms around him and grinned and made A finish the glass very quickly and said to Jack, i still remember that fucking time they suggested a motherfucking nigger what a fucking nerve fucking clam jousters, and suddenly A was feeling very tired and weary and dazed and confused and weak and then V snapped her fingers and Jack took A and carried him and they all three started climbing up the stairs to the second floor and Jack said, he wasnt a nigger he was maybe italian or maybe mexican or maybe brazilian you know or maybe argentinian or span, and V said to him, shut the fuck up fucking faggot, and she continued, i mean the notion that i would want to fuck a motherfucking cocksucking filthy nigger such fucking nerve for fucks sake, and Jack said, uh lets just focus on this little bitch for now, and V responded, shut the fuck up fucking faggot, and then she went on, at least they have never had the nerve to send a motherfucking kike cunt although i guess i would actually like that so i could fucking gas the fucking piece of shit beast rat cunt thatd be fucking great and maybe i would like to gas those two fucking clam jousters as well that would be so fucking fun, and then burst out with a very loud laughter and Jack looked just exhausted and A was still slightly conscious and as they all headed towards the huge bedroom Jack and V slept and fucked in A could see lots of photographs framed and hanging from the walls at the side of the stairs with some of them featuring Jack and V with a girl who looked to be around ten years old and a boy who looked to be around eight years old and they all had their mouths open very wide as if smiling or some stupid bullshit like that and they all looked like imbeciles and extremely stupid and pathetic and creepy in the extremely relevant and important opinion of A and when they entered the huge bedroom Jack and V slept and fucked in Jack placed A on the king size bed and above it hanging were a portrait of Myra Hindley and one of Karla Homolka and one Debra Lafave and one of Pamela Rogers Turner and one of Mary Kay Letourneau and one of Lorena Bobbitt and one of Mary Bell and one of Natasha Cornett and one of Shauna Hoare and one of Ilse Koch and one of Klara Mauerova and one of Aileen Wuornos and one of Jodi Arias and one of Leni Riefenstahl and one of Adolf Hitler and the Adolf Hitler portrait was the biggest and was the one that was at the center and there was also also a Nazi flag hanging with the swastika emblazoned on it and V went on, those dykes are just fucking insane and retarded fuck, and she had her nipples pierced and her cunt pierced and had swastika tattooed between her tits and then Jack and V opened a small safe box inside their gigantic closet and grabbed a huge bag of blow and opened it and started sniffing the blow and they were sniffing and sniffing and sniffing and sniffing and sniffing and sniffing and those were motherfucking mountains of fucking blow and neither of both assholes had the common courtesy of offering A at least a fucking miserable taste and at one point V got on all fours and ordered Jack to introduce some of it into her asshole with a little tube and after that V went to the bathroom and when she came back she was naked except for the black shoes with very fucking high heels and was carrying a lot of things among which were leather cuffs with which she very tightly tied A's wrists to the bedposts and then produced a ball gag and gagged A with it and then grabbed a black leather pig mask and put it on and adjusted it and secured it and then she put a big and pink strap on dildo on and then took a leather blindfold and blindfolded A with it and then fucked him with the big and pink strap on dildo and told him, up your ass, and A felt like he was being torn apart but he did not begin crying at all and V was saying, you like it little fag you love this little worthless slut fucking piece of shit faggot you love this youre nothing but an incomplete deformed dysfunctional lesser little girl you piece of shit, and slapped A over and over again and pinched and twisted his nipples and placed nipple clamps on them and pulled on them and produced a leather riding crop and began striking A with it and the pain was most definitely amongst the most excruciating A had ever felt and V continued striking him with the riding crop and she stroke and stroke and stroke and stroke and stroke and stroke and she kept penetrating her asshole with her fingers and moaning like a fucking idiot and took the ball gag out of A's mouth and then pulled out an used tampon out of her cunt and over the course of the next three hours V and Jack took turns fucking A, at one point V fucking Jack with the big and pink strap on dildo and hitting him with a black leather flogger on the back and she was hitting Jack very very fucking hard and the noises from the flogging could be heard all over the second floor and Jack was shrieking and in turn was fucking A and then A lost consciousness and when he woke up he was still on the bed face up and Jack's back was completely and absolutely and utterly red and adorned in some places with running blood and ripped pieces of flesh here and there and V wiped as much as possible of Jack's blood with her right hand and then smeared it on his face and then made him lick some of it and then she licked some of it smiling and then she tied A to the bed again and put the black blindfold on again and then touched the used tampon with her left hand and with her right hand began squashing A's scrotum and A started to whimper and pant and scream and V made him lick her menstrual blood smeared fingers on the threat that if he did not she would burst his testicles and she fucked A's mouth with her fingers very deep and almost introducing her whole hand and then she grabbed the tampon and continued squashing A's scrotum and made him put the entire tampon inside his mouth and suck on the blood and said, ive been thinking of making menstrual art lately what do you think, and eventually she got bored of that and took of the black leather pig mask and untied A and grabbed him and forced a black

leather mask that barely let him breathe at all over
his head and that had a dildo gag incorporated
inside and the thing covered his entire head and
he could hardly breathe at all and felt like he was
asphyxiating and V let the spaces for the eyes in
the mask open and started laughing out loud and
put A on a leash and handcuffed him and then he
was led by the leash by V and Jack to a room that
had a sign that read Germie with letters in the
colors of the rainbow at the door and A realized it
was the girl from the photographs and this was
her bedroom and Jack and V put him in a small
pink tutu that was inside the closet and then they
fucked him again for a long while and also made
him put a light blue dress with ribbons on it and
kept on fucking him for a long while and it was
extremely fucking painful as fuck and they did it
while they had A gagged with a pacifier gag with
leather straps which were very tightly tied around
his head and were making painful indents on his
skin and especially on his cheeks and were drawing
blood and the pacifier itself was pink and in the
shape of a very big heart and then suddenly V left
the room and very quickly came back with a tool
box fuck machine with a gargantuan dildo
attached to it and she and Jack then proceeded to

tie A up to the bed with plain metal cuffs this time and began fucking him with that tool box fuck machine with a gargantuan dildo attached to it and the pain was too much and too big for A and it was a taste of what was to come in the next following few years and then V and Jack took a pink and white stuffed hare from the floor and placed it just in front of A's left armpit and then began to take photographs and video of him and they were saying, smile precious little bitch, and they were laughing out loud and the pain was too much and too big for A and it was a taste of what was to come in the next following few years and for some reason all that time he had been restraining himself and all that effort he had been doing it were just annihilated and he finally gave up and suddenly an image of a teddy bear he had had as a small child and that had a big pink heart in its arms holding or embracing it came to his mind and then he began shedding tears and they were just really a few tears coming from reddened eyes and that only made V and Jack hysterically and maniacally begin to laugh out loud for what seemed like a motherfucking eternity and then when they got bored of that they let the cuffs off and dragged him completely naked and still

wearing the gag with the shape of a big pink heart
pacifier to the room of the boy and made him put
on a pair of boxer shorts that belonged to the boy
and obviously A immediately drenched them with
blood and V and Jack were still capturing
everything on video and photographs and they
were ordering him to pose in different ways while
wearing the blood drenched boxer shorts like
putting him on all fours on top of the bed with
hos ass and his eyes to the camera and also standing
with his arms behind his head looking at the
camera and then opposite to the camera with the
boxer shorts lowered showing completely his
bleeding ass cheeks and then again facing the
camera again with his arms behind his head with
the boxer shorts lowered just barely covering his
cock and balls and then another one like that but
with his hands cuffed and then various other ones
but completely naked this time including one
with V smiling and holding his cock and A
thought, what theyre gonna print and fucking
frame these photographs and fucking hang them
in their fucking walls or what the fuck, and after
all was over V and Jack handed him eighteen one
hundred dollar bills of which he was to give not a
single fucking one to Eve and Illona because they

had been given their cut in advance and A was thinking of all of this as he was riding the subway and Blouse were saying in his earphones, counting off our loss you know it stays for winter and then the tears flow youve never been the same since you hit the ground well welcome to the last stand, and then he got off the subway and it had been good since only two assholes and one bitch had grabbed his ass or rubbed his crotch and he walked and walked and walked and walked and thought about all the people that propositioned him on a daily basis all the old and young and fat and slender and hot and cute and ugly and ugly as fuck and rich and poor and poor as fuck and homeless and short and tall and all that shit and he could not give a shit about it all if a life long free supply of Oxys depended on it and all of those thoughts made him all of a sudden aware of his now always completely chronically and preternaturally limp cock and suddenly he felt like throwing up but did not and then someone ran their hand all over his crotch and his balls and his cock and his chest and his nipples and squeezed and it was a very pale woman with very red and very wild and long hair and dressed in black and with green eyes and with a lot of black mascara on and A was just startled and finally got off of the subway and looked behind him and the woman was standing up smiling at him with an insane and wide as fuck smile and then A just fucking walked and walked and walked and finally got to school at Forty Second Street and went in and somewhere some dude was somewhat loudly listening to the Foo Fighters who were saying, seems my time is growing thin, and A tried to take a look at the dude but his hair was covering his face completely and so A went to see this teacher of his and old him he hadn't read the motherfucking book and hadn't written the motherfucking subsequent paper and the teacher informed him he therefore had failed the class and A got up and got out with the idiot still talking and he went out to the street again and headed towards the Village and passed Generation Records and got to the cafe where the meeting with the loser had been set and he sat outside and the loser was already there and looked to be maybe ten years older than A and actually was holding a Generation Records bag and it turned out A was right and the loser got up and was stupidly smiling and shook the extremely soft hand A barely extended and told him how glad he was that A had really made it and how he thought and was afraid he was not going to show up at all and that maybe he had forgotten all about it and the loser was blushing so bad A almost felt embarrassed for him and then the waiter came to their table and the loser ordered a Coke and A did the same and the loser then said how cool and how great it was that they were both going to drink the same and A just said something like, yeah, ive been drinking coke every day for almost all my life, very quietly in a whisper, and the loser kind of smiled and said, me too, and then when the waiter came back with their cokes the loser clinked his glass with the one A had and they both drank and talked for a little while about A and his fucking tumblr and Instagram fucking accounts and photography and about how was school going and about how he was doing and to A almost everything was white noise and he replied to all the questions with all the monosyllables that came to his mind at the moment and after all that he got up and excused himself uttering some bullshit with the loser looking sad and disappointed like a little child being abandoned and finally they both shook hands and said their goodbyes with the loser wishing him a great day or week or whatever the fuck and saying how great it would be if they could do this again and A just nodded and then he left knowing as he was leaving that the guy was actually fucking crying afterwards which was of course the kind of shit he could not be bothered with and so he just walked and walked and walked and walked and walked and walked and walked and walked and walked and walked and walked and walked and walked and walked and walked and walked and walked and walked like in a daze and he passed the Washington Hotel in Third Avenue and after a long while of still walking and walking and walking and walking and walking and walking he passed Rainbow Fashions and that disgusting and old and filthy building where that old witch whore Domino had once lived and after a while he found himself in a street he did not know at all and he was walking and to his left there was an old couple and the man taller than the woman and he had his left hand on her left shoulder and they both looked at him with what seemed to A to be surprise and disgust and he kept on walking and to his right he encountered an old man with sunglasses and a black hat and the man stared at him as he walked past him and A kept on walking and there was a mirror and he looked at his reflection and when he turned around there was a very pale woman with very red and very wild and long hair and dressed in black and with green eyes and with a lot of black mascara on and A realized it was the woman from the subway and she said to him, hey boy, and tried to grab him and he moved away from her and she followed him and continued, take a look at me, and again she tried to grab him and she put her arms around A and drew him down to her so she could make him touch her breasts all perfume and A was going mad and again he tried to move away and he managed to very quickly free himself of her but this time he lost his balance and fell to the pavement where the cars were passing not seeing the huge garbage truck being driven by an utterly shitfaced drunk guy that was coming his way and ran him over and he just ended up there on the pavement and that was it, with his guts spilled, his crushed belly with death inside of it, the deadest of the dead.

www.ingramcontent.com/pod-product-compliance
Lightning Source LLC
Chambersburg PA
CBHW030355180626
46812CB00007B/2885

* 9 7 8 1 6 0 8 6 4 1 3 6 9 *